I Wish I Was an Alien

READZ NE

Readzone Books Limited

First published in this edition 2015

© in this edition ReadZone Books Limited 2015
© in text Vivian French 2005
© in illustrations Lisa Williams 2005

Vivian French has asserted her right under the Copyright Designs and Patents Act 1988 to be identified as the author of this work.

Lisa Williams has asserted her right under the Copyright Designs and Patents Act 1988 to be identified as the illustrator of this work.

Every attempt has been made by the Publisher to secure appropriate permissions for material reproduced in this book. If there has been any oversight we will be happy to rectify the situation in future editions or reprints. Written submissions should be made to the Publisher.

British Library Cataloguing in Publication Data (CIP) is available for this title.

Printed in Malta by Melita Press.

ISBN 978 1 78322 413 5

Visit our website: www.readzonebooks.com

I Wish I Was an Alien

by Vivian French

illustrated by Lisa Williams

I wouldn't wash my face.

I'd fly around the planets...

...and I'd zoom around the stars.

I'd go and check out Jupiter.

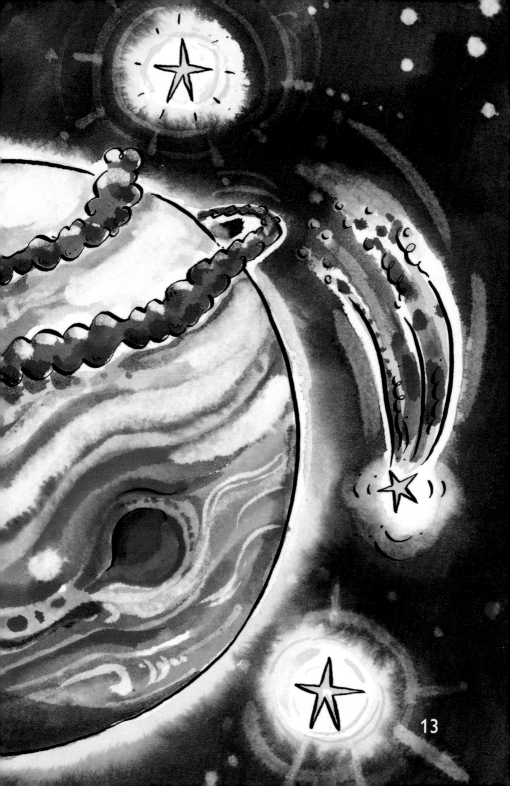

13

I wish I was a boy on Earth and didn't live in space. I wouldn't have these tentacles, instead I'd have a face.

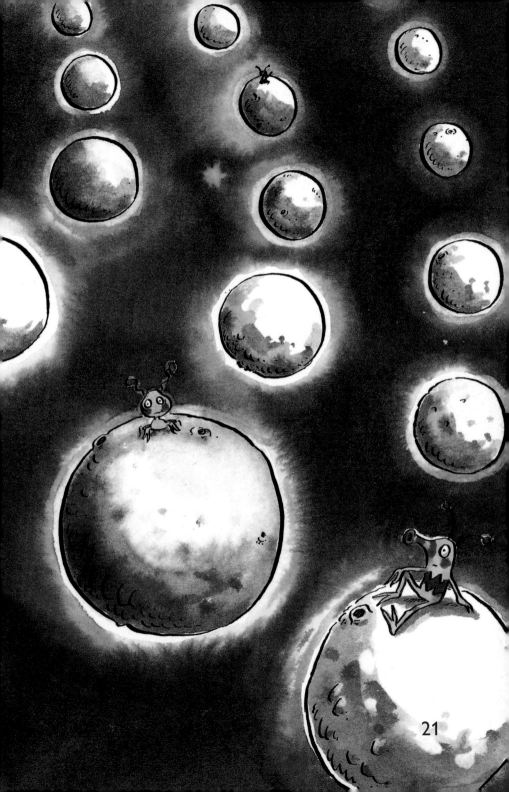

26

...and I want to go to school.